Dear Parent:
Your child's love of re

Every child learns to read in a different way and at his or her own speed. Some go back and forth between reading levels and read favorite books again and again. Others read through each level in order. You can help your young reader improve and become more confident by encouraging his or her own interests and abilities. From books your child reads with you to the first books he or she reads alone, there are I Can Read Books for every stage of reading:

SHARED READING
Basic language, word repetition, and whimsical illustrations, ideal for sharing with your emergent reader

BEGINNING READING
Short sentences, familiar words, and simple concepts for children eager to read on their own

READING WITH HELP
Engaging stories, longer sentences, and language play for developing readers

READING ALONE
Complex plots, challenging vocabulary, and high-interest topics for the independent reader

I Can Read Books have introduced children to the joy of reading since 1957. Featuring award-winning authors and illustrators and a fabulous cast of beloved characters, I Can Read Books set the standard for beginning readers.

A lifetime of discovery begins with the magical words **"I Can Read!"**

Visit www.icanread.com for information
on enriching your child's reading experience.

*To everyone out there with
big dreams—you can do it!
—Girl Scouts*

*For my sister, Ashley—
tenacious, funny, and wiser
than I'd like to admit.
—T.E.*

**Want to join the fun?
Ask an adult to use this QR code
to access fun activities, earn patches, and
see what being a Girl Scout is all about!**

HarperCollins Children's Books, a division of HarperCollins Publishers,
195 Broadway, New York, NY 10007

HarperCollins Publishers, Macken House, 39/40 Mayor Street Upper, Dublin 1, D01 C9W8, Ireland

I Can Read® and I Can Read Book® are trademarks of HarperCollins Publishers

The Amazing Daisies
Copyright © 2026 by Girl Scouts of the United States of America
The Girl Scouts® name and all associated marks and logotypes, including Trefoil design, are registered trademarks of GSUSA.
All rights reserved. Manufactured in Johor, Malaysia.
No part of this book may be used or reproduced in any manner whatsoever without written permission except in the case of brief quotations embodied in critical articles and reviews. Without limiting the exclusive rights of any author, contributor, or the publisher of this publication, any unauthorized use of this publication to train generative artificial intelligence (AI) technologies is expressly prohibited. HarperCollins also exercises their rights under Article 4(3) of the Digital Single Market Directive 2019/790 and expressly reserves this publication from the text and data mining exception.
harpercollins.com

Library of Congress Control Number: 2025940658
ISBN 978-0-06-331790-1 (trade bdg.) — 978-0-06-331789-5 (pbk.)

Book design by Stephanie Hays

25 26 27 28 29 PCA 10 9 8 7 6 5 4 3 2 1   First Edition

girl scouts

THE AMAZING DAISIES

pictures by Tiffany Everett

HARPER
An Imprint of HarperCollinsPublishers

Daisy Lane is the best street.

An amazing street!

At least,

Ava thought so.

Daisy Lane has ten homes,

all different colors.

Daisy Lane has shady trees

and lots of flowers.

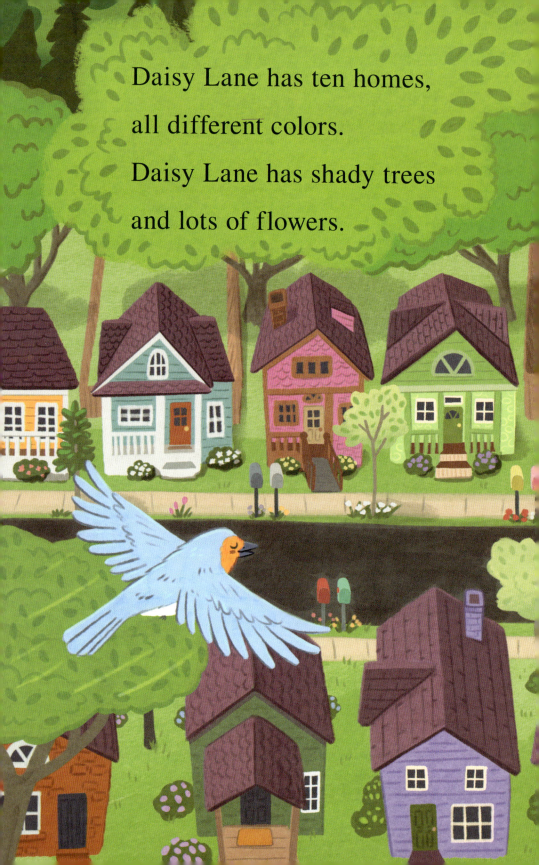

Daisy Lane even has a playground!

And Daisy Lane

has the best neighbors,

like Ava's friends from Girl Scouts,

Ellie and Hazel!

One day, they all met up

for games and snacks.

But Daisy Lane did not have
a recycling bin.

10

"Let's get one for the playground. Maybe our Daisy Girl Scout troop can raise the money," said Ava.

"Then Daisy Lane will be even more amazing," said Ellie.

Ava, Ellie, and Hazel told
their Girl Scout troop the idea.

"We need to sell forty boxes
of Girl Scout Cookies.
Then we'll have enough money
for the recycling bin," said Hazel.

12

The troop agreed!

The next day,

Ava, Ellie, and Hazel got to work.

First they set up a cookie booth

at the playground.

Ava is an artist.

She made two big posters.

HELP US BUY A RECYCLIN'

Ellie loves music.

She wrote a song.

"You buy a box.

We'll buy a bin.

Together we can all pitch in!"

the friends sang.

A kid and mom stopped by.

They bought two boxes.

"It's working!" said Hazel.

Hazel's big sister, Ariel,
bought one.

"Amazing setup!" Ariel said.

They sold two more boxes
to two dog walkers.
"Amazing idea!" they said.

The friends sold cookies
all afternoon.

"Give a box as a gift," said Hazel.

"Eat some for a snack," said Ava.

"Buy one to help us
get a bin!" said Ellie.

The day wore on.

Sales slowed down.

Only five boxes were left.

But the goal was to sell them all.

Ellie sang her song again.

Ava waved a poster.

The last two kids at the playground each bought one!

But now it was quiet.

Everyone had gone home for dinner.

The friends looked down.

Three boxes.

Three of them.

They pulled money

from their pockets.

They each bought a box
and ate some cookies!

They had done it!

Daisy Lane would get

its recycling bin.

It would be even more amazing!

Just like them—

Ellie, Ava, and Hazel.

The Amazing Daisies!

Junk to Jewelry

There are many fun ways to recycle! One way is to turn scrap paper and other trash into jewelry. You can make something for yourself or a friend!

Materials

- scrap paper, bottle caps and/or pull tabs from soda cans (be careful with sharp edges), scissors, glue, or tape

- optional: crayons, markers, paint, and stickers

Let's get creative!

1 With an adult's help, cut a rectangular strip from the paper that's long enough to be a bracelet or necklace.

2 Color the paper any way you'd like.

Add stickers if you'd like.

3 Paint bottle caps or pull tabs to make pendants.

4 Glue or tape the pendants to the paper.

5 Glue or tape one end of the paper to the other.

You have a **ONE-OF-A-KIND** necklace or bracelet!